Text copyright © Victoria Brotherton 2019
Illustrations copyright © Billie Hastie 2019
All rights reserved.
ISBN: 978-1-912655-30-4

First published 2019
by Rowanvale Books Ltd
The Gate
Keppoch Street
Roath
Cardiff
CF24 3JW
www.rowanvalebooks.com
Library Cataloguing in Publication Data.
A catalogue record for this book is available from the British Library.

For my two boys, love always.

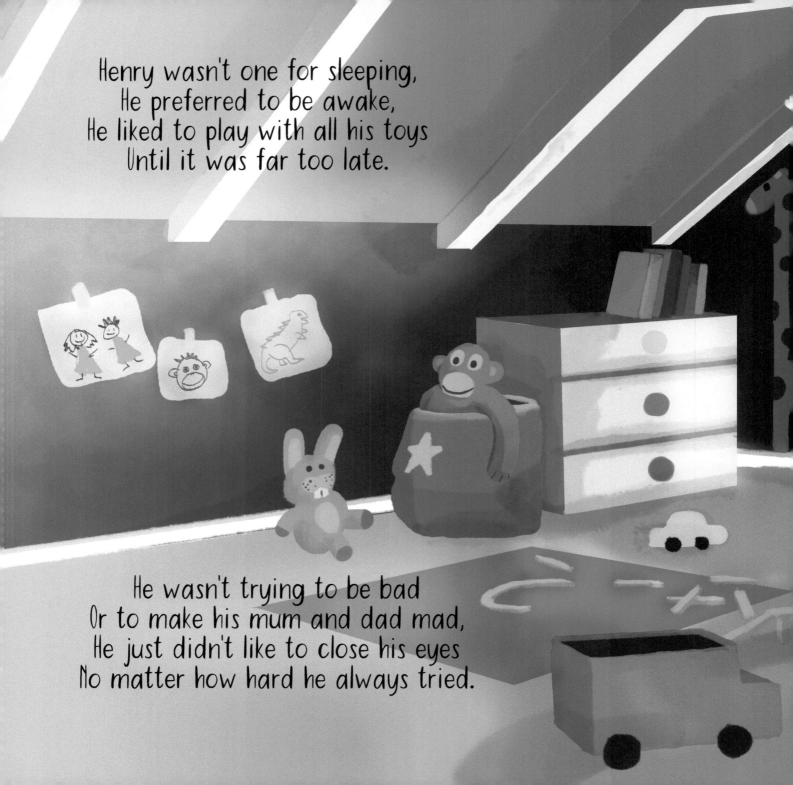

Henry wasn't one for sleeping,
He preferred to be awake,
He liked to play with all his toys
Until it was far too late.

He wasn't trying to be bad
Or to make his mum and dad mad,
He just didn't like to close his eyes
No matter how hard he always tried.

He was far too busy to go to bed;
Adventures of the day always filled his head.
Worried that he would be missing out,
"Snoring's boring!" he would shout.

After several verses of his favourite song
And his chosen book, that was far too long,
Mum kissed him goodnight and turned for the door,
Tiptoeing and leaping over creaks in the floor.

But as soon as the door began to close,
Henry shot up from his dream-like doze.
He cried so hard he started to choke
And when Mum gave in, he softly spoke.

"I can't sleep, I won't sleep,
I wish that you could see,
I've really really tried to sleep,
But sleep's just not for me."

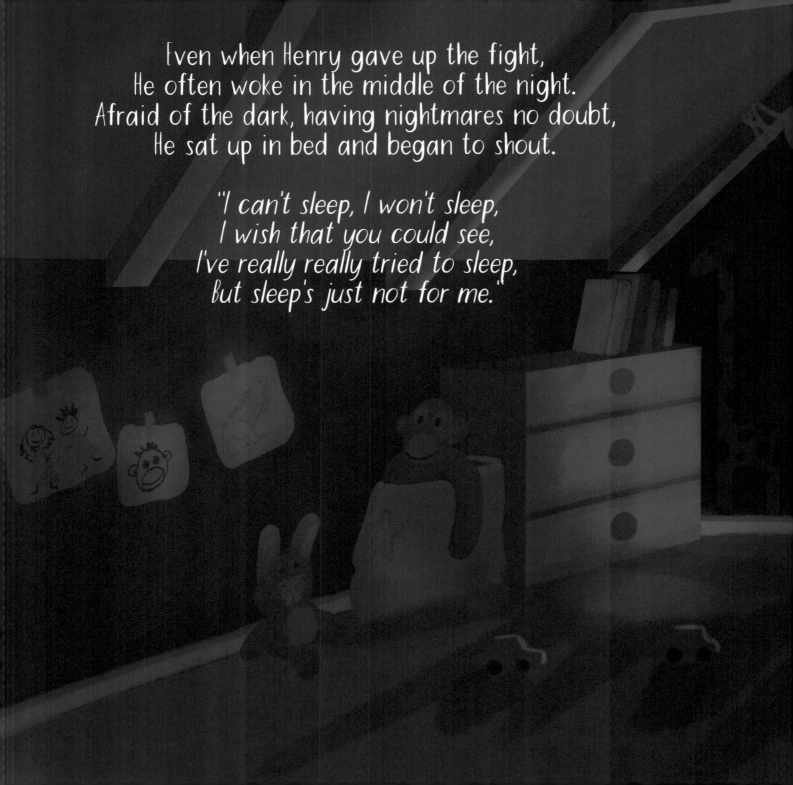

Even when Henry gave up the fight,
He often woke in the middle of the night.
Afraid of the dark, having nightmares no doubt,
He sat up in bed and began to shout.

"I can't sleep, I won't sleep,
I wish that you could see,
I've really really tried to sleep,
But sleep's just not for me."

Mum and Dad struggled to open their eyes
On the days that Henry would wake at five.
Desperate for rest, he moved into their bed,
Elbowing and rolling into Dad's head.

Henry tried anything to avoid going to sleep:
"I want a hug, I need a wee, and where is Mr Sheep?"
Wide awake and feeling all alone,
He stood at his door and started to moan.

"I can't sleep, I won't sleep,
I wish that you could see,
I've really really tried to sleep,
But sleep's just not for me."

But when it was time to get up the next day,
It was impossible to wake him from where he lay.
The morning routine was always rushed,
So he'd leave the house with his hair unbrushed!

At school, Henry missed out on quite a lot.
He even nodded off on his carpet spot,
Only waking to the school cockerel's crow,
As it wandered around outside
the class window!

Henry's teacher, Mrs Bright,
Would often say, "Get an early night."
But because he was just a little bit shy,
He'd shake his head and quietly reply...

On Monday he slept through his morning break;

In art on Tuesday he couldn't stay awake;

On Wednesday, he missed
his lunchtime play;

He dozed off in singing
practice on
Thursday.

By Friday, Henry was too tired to speak,
But this was his favourite day of the week.
A school trip left him feeling very excited,
A class of small faces left school delighted.

Eventually the
bus pulled up
at the zoo
And Henry
was partnered
with Max,
who was new.

They gazed
at the animals,
from monkeys
to bats,
Until they
arrived at
the den for
big cats.

Henry peered through the thick barrier glass,
And spotted the lion asleep on the grass!
His smile faded and he muttered,
"Snoring's boring."
But the lion woke up and started roaring.

"I don't spend all my time lying down,
I'm king of the jungle and I wear a crown.
I am strong, I am powerful, and Louis is my name,
I'm courageous and fierce, just look at my mane."

Max wandered off, not hearing a thing,
But an open-mouthed Henry still stared at the king.
The lion yawned, "I need lots of sleep, up to twenty hours a day,
Without which I couldn't catch my prey."

"I laze around all day to hunt at night,
That's how I get my energy and might.
And when the day's work is done,
I prowl back to my pride to be the protective one."

And as quick as he spoke, he skulked away,
As Mrs Bright tried to take her class home for the day.
On the bus, Henry thought of the lion, so bold, fierce and strong:
No wonder they call him the powerful one!

Yawning, Henry lay in bed that night,
Still trying to put up the same old fight,
But the words of the lion, spoken
that day,
Rang in his ears as he started to say...

"I can't sleep, I won't sleep,
I wish that you could see,
I've really really
tried to sleep..."

...And he slept so quietly!

Author Profile

Victoria Brotherton is a primary school teacher and mother to two young boys. Her books are based on her experiences both as a teacher and a parent and they are written to inspire and ignite imagination. Victoria is a strong believer in imagination being the door to possibilities.

Follow more of Victoria Brotherton's work on Instagram @brothertonbooks

Publisher Information

Rowanvale Books provides publishing services to independent authors, writers and poets all over the globe. We deliver a personal, honest and efficient service that allows authors to see their work published, while remaining in control of the process and retaining their creativity. By making publishing services available to authors in a cost-effective and ethical way, we at Rowanvale Books hope to ensure that the local, national and international community benefits from a steady stream of good quality literature.

For more information about us, our authors or our publications, please get in touch.
www.rowanvalebooks.com
info@rowanvalebooks.com